SCARY!
David Orme

Contents

The scary book

One night, Ben, Tanya and Luke
were in the shed in Luke's garden.

Tanya was reading a history book.
Ben was reading a football book.
Luke was reading a book
about space monsters!

It was a very scary book.
It had a green spotty monster
on the front.

SCARY!

David Orme

Illustrated by Robin Lawrie

Titles in First Flight

Badger Publishing Limited
15 Wedgwood Gate, Pin Green Industrial Estate,
Stevenage, Hertfordshire SG1 4SU
Telephone: 01438 356907. Fax: 01438 747015
www.badger-publishing.co.uk
enquiries@badger-publishing.co.uk

Scary ISBN 1 84424 820 8

Series Editor: Jonny Zucker
Publisher: David Jamieson
Commissioning Editor: Carrie Lewis
Editor: Paul Martin
Design: Fiona Grant
Illustration: Robin Lawrie

Luke liked reading
about scary things.

He didn't like it when people
scared him!

"It says here that space monsters visit the Earth," said Luke. "Sometimes they take people into space."

"That is rubbish," said Ben. "I don't know anyone who has been taken away by a space monster."

"That is because they never come back," said Luke.

Just then they heard a noise.

The scary noise

It was a big, scary noise coming from outside the shed.

"That sounds horrible!" said Ben.

"That sounds like a spaceship!" said Luke.

"How do you know what spaceships sound like?" asked Tanya.

"Well, I don't," said Luke. "But I bet it is one!"

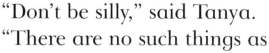

"Don't be silly," said Tanya. "There are no such things as space monsters."

"Well, why don't you get up and look out of the window then," said Ben.

"I don't want to," said Tanya. "You look if you want to."

"Why should I?"

"Well, it was your idea."

Just then they saw a light,
shining through the window.

A short and scary chapter

It was a flashing, blue light.

Tanya was afraid. Why did Luke have to talk about space monsters? There was no such thing!

Or was there?

"Spaceships have flashing lights!"
said Luke. "They flash them
when they are going to
grab somebody!"

Just then they heard footsteps
outside.

Scary – and hairy!

The footsteps came closer.
Closer.
Closer.

Luke, Ben and Tanya did not move.

Then something even more scary
happened, and I mean really scary.
Are you ready for this?

A thing with big eyes was looking at them through the window.

It was very scary.
And very hairy.

"It is a space monster!" gasped Ben.

"I don't want to be grabbed by a space monster!" sobbed Tanya. "I want to read my book!"

"Perhaps you can take it into space with you," said Ben. "I wonder if they play football in space?"

Just then there was a noise.

Even scarier

It was a bang.

BANG

Just like that.
On the door.
Slowly, the door cre-e-e-eaked
open. A yellow light shone into the
shed . . .

And someone . . .or something . . .
looked in . . .

"Hello gang!" said the policeman. "I'm looking for a lost dog. Have you seen one?"

"What does it look like?" asked Ben.

"It's hairy," said the policeman.

"How hairy?" said Luke.

"Very hairy."

"Is it as hairy as that one?" asked Tanya.

A very hairy dog was looking through the window.

"I would say it's just about that hairy. In fact, that is the dog I'm looking for," said the policeman.

"Thanks for your help, gang. There is a reward for the person who finds the dog. That must be all of you."

"What is the reward?" asked Ben.

"It's a trip to the cinema, to see that new film about space monsters," said the policeman. "It's really scary!"

"I don't think I will like it," said Tanya.

Soon the policeman went off with the dog.

Ben and Tanya told Luke to stop scaring them about Space Monsters.

"But it could have been a space monster!" said Luke, laughing.
But Ben and Tanya didn't think it was funny.

"Don't be silly," they said. "Space monsters DON'T EXIST!"
But Luke didn't believe them.

They all started to read their books again.

Outside the shed, it was a dark, cloudy night.

High above the shed, hidden in the clouds, was a spaceship. Inside it was a very strange creature.

It was green and spotty, with loads of eyes, just like the one on the cover of Luke's book.

He liked dark, cloudy nights. They were perfect for grabbing people and taking them off into space.

He wondered who might be down below, waiting to be grabbed.

He looked down. Aha, a shed!
The green and spotty creature
turned on his alien x-ray and
looked through the roof.

"AAAGHHHH!"

I bet you can't guess who made
that noise. Well, it was the green
spotty alien. He had seen Tanya
and Ben and Luke.

He had never seen anything that
looked as scary as them.

They only had two eyes.
They weren't green.
They didn't have any spots.

"AAAGHHHH!"
(That was him again.)

The monster from space flew back into space as fast as he could.

"This planet is much too scary," he said.